Little Polyglot Adventures

A Multicultural Picnic

Written by
Victor D. O. Santos

Illustrated by
Eszter Miklós

Little Polyglot Adventures (series)
Book 3: A Multicultural Picnic
English Edition

(companion to Book 1: Dylan's Birthday Present, Book 2: A Wild Day at the Zoo, & Book 4: Kiki Goes to Brazil)

Written by: Victor Dias de Oliveira Santos
Illustrations: Eszter Miklós
Layout: César Pires de Almeida

ISBN: 978-1-64962-091-0 (paperback)
ISBN: 978-1-64962-092-7 (hardcover)

City of Publication: Urbandale, IA, USA

Published by Linguacious®

www.linguacious.net
email: contact@linguacious.net

This book is also available in a coloring-book version
(ISBN: 978-1-64962-097-2)

 www.facebook.com/linguacious

 www.twitter.com/linguacious_llc

 www.instagram.com/linguacious_llc

Foreign words in this book

You will come across six words/expressions in different languages while reading this book. To listen to how they are pronounced, simply access the link below:

linguacious.net/lpa-audio

or scan this QR code:

"One language sets you in a corridor for life. Two languages open every door along the way."

– Frank Smith

"Wake up, Dylan! We're going to be late for our picnic!" shouted Isabella as she jumped up and down on her brother's bed.

"Just one hundred more minutes…" replied Dylan, covering his head with a pillow.

"Okay, I will tell our grandparents you don't want to come," Isabella teased as she left Dylan's bedroom.

Dylan sprung out of bed faster than a monkey when it sees a banana, threw on his favorite Ukrainian T-shirt, and headed for the living room.

His three grandparents had arrived the night before, and the family always had a picnic to celebrate their arrival. Dylan loved seeing his grandparents each year and cherished every opportunity to speak Portuguese and Ukrainian with them.

"Vamos, queridos[1]," **Grandma Elisa said in Portuguese. "We will have the best picnic ever!"**

"We are taking so much food that we could open our own supermarket at the park. Дивись![2] **" joked Grandma Valentyna, speaking in Ukrainian.**

1   *This means "Let's go, my darlings" in Portuguese.*
2   *This means "Look!" in Ukrainian.*

The whole family, including Kiki, Dylan's pet chicken, left for the park.

At the park, they met Dylan's best friend, Emma, and her parents. Dylan and Emma hugged and helped put all the food on the picnic blanket.

There were all kinds of food: American, Ukrainian, Brazilian, and even a South African dish called *bobotie* that Emma's parents had made.

The two families ate and chatted for a long time. People passing by could hear them speaking in English, Ukrainian, Portuguese, and Zulu.

Across the park, a group of boys couldn't stop staring and giggling at the group.

"Let's go play with my remote-control car!" Dylan said to Emma and Isabella. The three kids ran to a large, open area in the park. Dylan turned on his car and made it zigzag across the field. Kiki started to run after the car, like a cat chasing a mouse.

"In the last two minutes, Kiki got more exercise than I do in an entire week," joked Dylan and Isabella's dad, looking at the kids playing in the distance.

The boys who had been staring at them came closer. In front of the group was a tall boy.

"Where did you get that funny-looking T-shirt? A museum?" All the other boys started to laugh. "And in what weird language were you talking to those people over there?" asked the boy. "And why do the two of you hang out together?"

"Leave him alone," Emma said. "His T-shirt is beautiful and handmade. It's not something you can buy at a cheap store. And he can speak more languages than any of us, which is really cool. Please, leave us alone."

The boys left, giggling like little hyenas.

Dylan, Emma, Isabella, and Kiki continued playing with the toy car.

Suddenly, they heard a boy yell out angrily from the distance.

"Stop it! Stop it!"

Emma, Dylan, and Isabella ran to see what was happening.

They found the tall boy from before sitting in a puddle of mud on the ground. His T-shirt was so dirty that they couldn't read any of the words on it. His friends were laughing uncontrollably at him.

"You can wipe yourself with this towel," said Emma.

"And you can wear my T-shirt if you want," said Dylan, taking off his favorite Ukrainian T-shirt. "I have another one underneath it."

The tall boy couldn't believe what was happening. He had been quite mean to Dylan and Emma just a few minutes ago, but here they were, helping him.

The boy cleaned himself with the towel and changed into Dylan's T-shirt.

"I am sorry I said those things to you. My name is Lee. You know… I am also different. My parents come from China and speak Mandarin to me at home. I don't tell this secret to other kids because I don't want to seem different, but I can trust you because you are different like me. Oh, and xiè xie (谢谢)[1] for the T-shirt. It's actually pretty nice."

"Дякую[2]," replied Dylan in Ukrainian. "Lee, let me introduce you to my polyglot chicken. She is also different from most other chickens."

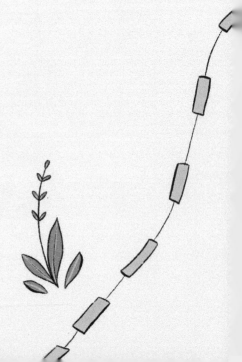

---

1 *This means "Thank you" in Mandarin.*
2 *This means "Thank you" in Ukrainian.*

When Dylan looked around, he could not see Kiki.

He asked his family and Emma's if they had seen her, but no one knew where Kiki was.

"We left her right here when we went to see why you were screaming. What if someone took her away?" asked Emma nervously.

"I have an idea!" said Lee. "You helped me when I needed help. Now it's my turn to return the favor. Do you have a cell phone?"

"Um… a cell phone?" asked Dylan, surprised. "I don't think calling Kiki will work…"

"No, you silly," replied Lee with a smile. "I need a phone to find Kiki."

"Um… okay…" said Dylan, still confused.

He went to find his grandpa and brought Grandpa's phone to Lee.

Lee pressed some buttons and the phone started to play chick sounds. Cheep! Cheep! Then he attached the cell phone to Dylan's toy car with a string and started to drive the car around the park.

Suddenly, something jumped out of a bush.

It was Kiki! She started to chase the car at full speed, thinking it was a chick that needed her help! Lee brought the car to a stop near Dylan's feet. Kiki followed behind it, still pecking at the car.

"You found Kiki! Thank you, Lee!" Dylan said. "You are a genius!"

Dylan, Emma, and Isabella invited Lee to join their picnic and asked him to teach them some words in Mandarin.

Lee looked around and started to point at things, saying their name in Mandarin. *"Qiú (球)!¹ Wán jù (玩具)!²"*

Dylan, Emma and Isabella repeated the words out loud.

---

1   *This means "ball" in Mandarin.*
2   *This means "toy" in Mandarin.*

"Wow! You guys have no foreign accent when you speak Mandarin! How do you do that?!"

"I guess knowing other languages helps us learn new ones," replied Isabella. "It makes us special, like it makes you special too."

Dylan's and Emma's families smiled. They were proud of the kind, multilingual, and multicultural kids they were raising.

From that day on, Lee was often seen playing with Dylan, Emma, and Isabella. And on some days, he even wore a traditional Chinese T-shirt he got from his parents...

CPSIA information can be obtained
at www.ICGtesting.com
Printed in the USA
LVHW052106090921
697455LV00006B/230